© 1995 Geddes & Grosset Ltd
Published by Geddes & Grosset Ltd,
New Lanark, Scotland.

ISBN 1 85534 592 7

Printed and bound in Great Britain.

The Enormous Turnip

Retold by Judy Hamilton
Illustrated by R. James Binnie

Tarantula Books

There once lived an old man and his wife who took great pride in the vegetables that they grew in their garden. They grew enough for themselves to eat and some more as well. The extra vegetables were shared among the other people that lived nearby. The vegetables were always large, healthy specimens and the old man and his wife had every right to be proud of them.

Every year in springtime, the old couple would sit down together to decide what to grow in their garden that year. One year, as well as the usual potatoes and carrots, cabbages and onions, they decided to grow turnips.

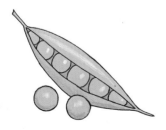

The old man and his wife set to work, digging the soil and planting the seeds with care. It was hard work, but they knew that they would be rewarded with a lovely crop of vegetables.

Last of all, the old couple planted the turnip seeds.

"I hope we get a good crop from these," said the old man to his wife.

"I am sure that we shall," his wife assured him.

They watered the sowing ground and settled down to wait for the seeds to grow.

Some weeks later, the seedlings began to emerge from the earth. All of the vegetables were growing well, but one turnip seedling was shooting up faster than the rest.

The old man and his wife tended their crops with the usual care and the turnip seedling which had shot up from the ground continued to grow faster and bigger than all the others. Every day when the old couple went to look at their garden, the turnip had doubled in size! Weeks later, the turnips were ready to pick and the old man and his wife pulled them from the ground one by one as they needed them. It was a great crop and they were able to give many away to friends and neighbours. But they left the biggest turnip in the ground. It continued to grow and soon it was quite enormous. Its leaves stood tall and its top swelled in a great mound above the ground.

Eventually, all the turnips in the garden had been picked except for the enormous turnip. It stayed where it was, casting a shadow on the garden around it. Then one day the old lady came to her husband and said:

"I would like to make soup today. It is time to pull up the enormous turnip."

So the old man went out into the garden and began to pull the enormous turnip top. He pulled and pulled as hard as he could, but the turnip would not move at all. So he called to his wife:

"I cannot pull this turnip up all by myself. You will have to come and help me."

The old lady came out to help. She pulled the old man and the old man pulled the turnip.

The old lady and the old man pulled and pulled at the enormous turnip as hard as they could, but still it would not move at all. So they went to ask a boy who lived nearby to come and help.

"We cannot pull up the enormous turnip by ourselves," they said. "Please come and help us."

So the boy came into the garden to help. He pulled the old lady, the old lady pulled the old man and the old man pulled the turnip. The boy and the old lady and the old man pulled and pulled as hard as they could but still the enormous turnip would not move at all. They knew that they would have to get more help, so the boy went to call his sister.

"We cannot pull up the enormous turnip by ourselves," said the boy. "Please come and help us."

So the girl came into the garden to help. She pulled the boy, the boy pulled the old lady, the old lady pulled the old man and the old man pulled the turnip. The girl and the boy and the old lady and the old man pulled and pulled as hard as they could but still the enormous turnip would not move. They needed more help, so the girl and the boy went off to call their father.

"We cannot pull up the enormous turnip by ourselves," they said. "Please come and help us."

So the father of the boy and the girl came into the garden to help.

The father pulled the girl, the girl pulled the boy, the boy pulled the old lady, the old lady pulled the old man and the old man pulled the turnip. The father and the girl and the boy and the old lady and the old man pulled and pulled as hard as they could, but still the enormous turnip would not move at all.

"This really is an enormous turnip," said the old man. "We have pulled and pulled as hard as we can and yet it will not budge. What can we do now?"

"We will have to find some more help," said the old lady. "We have to get this turnip out of the ground so that I can make my soup."

The father of the boy and girl went to get his horse to help. The horse was big and strong and used to hard work.

"We cannot pull up this turnip by ourselves," he said. "You will have to come and help."

So he brought the horse into the garden to help. The horse pulled the father, the father pulled the girl, the girl pulled the boy, the boy pulled the old lady, the old lady pulled the old man and the old man pulled the turnip. The horse and the father and the girl and the boy and the old lady and the old man pulled and pulled as hard as they could, but still the enormous turnip would not move.

"I think this turnip is stuck here for ever," said the old man.

"We cannot leave the turnip in the ground," said the old lady. "If it gets any bigger, there will be no more room for the other vegetables in the garden. Besides, I want to make my soup!"

"Then there is nothing else for it," said the old man. "We will have to find some more help!"

They all looked around to see if there was anyone nearby who could come and help them, but there was nobody to be seen. Then the old man remembered his cross old billy goat, who was tethered in the field next to the garden.

"The billy goat will have to come and help us," said the old man.

The billy goat was a very bad-tempered animal, and the old man was not sure if he could get it to help them, but he asked it very politely:

"We cannot pull up the enormous turnip by ourselves. Please come and help us."

The billy goat had been watching the turnip grow for a very long time and thought that it looked quite delicious. If he helped to pull it out of the ground, he might be able to get a tasty piece for supper. He still looked very cross, but he let the old man lead him into the garden.

Licking his lips at the sight of the enormous turnip, he went over to help the others.

The goat pulled the horse, the horse pulled the father, the father pulled the girl, the girl pulled the boy, the boy pulled the old lady, the old lady pulled the old man and the old man pulled the turnip. The goat and the horse and the father and the girl and the boy and the old lady and the old man pulled as hard as they could. They pulled some more. The turnip moved! They pulled again. The turnip moved a bit more! They pulled and pulled and PULLED......

"POP!"

The turnip shot out of the ground.

The old man, the old lady, the boy, the girl, the father, the horse and the billy goat fell on top of each other in a breathless heap.